Eleanor, Ellatony, Ellencake, and Me

By C.M. Rubin
Illustrated by Christopher Fowler

GINGHAM DOG
P R E S S

Columbus, Ohio

To my Mother for her inspirational creativity
Thank you Harry, Gabriella, and James for
your love and support
Cathy

To Tina, Maggie, Molly, and Micki
Chris

Children's Publishing

This edition published in the United States of America in 2003 by
Gingham Dog Press
an imprint of McGraw-Hill Children's Publishing,
a Division of The McGraw-Hill Companies
8787 Orion Place
Columbus, Ohio 43240-4027

www.MHkids.com

Library of Congress Cataloging-in-Publication Data is on file with the publisher.

Printed in The United States of America.

1-57768-412-5

1 2 3 4 5 6 7 8 9 10 PHXBK 09 08 07 06 05 04 03

The McGraw-Hill Companies

My Life began with just one name—
Eleanor!
That's all,
No more.
Just
Eleanor.

One girl, one name, it sounds okay.
But things did not work out that way.
My name kept changing every day.

Each member of
my family
soon had a different
name for me.
And with that name
perhaps a dream
about the girl
that I will be.

Nana says I'm very witty,
precious, poised, polite, and pretty
slender, stylish, smart, and sweet,
nimble, natural, nice, and neat.
WOW!
However,
she says she finds it such a bore
to call her grandchild Eleanor.

Since Nana's Nana came from France,
she thinks my name needs more "romance."
She calls me Elle,
her precious belle,
her pretty, poised mademoiselle.

The fashion world's latest creation was draped upon its new sensation, the slender, stylish model Elle, that pretty, poised mademoiselle.

But dearie me,
catastrophe!
The big hat tipped!
And mademoiselle,
it seems she fell!
It seems she tripped!

So sad, too bad,
for poor belle Elle.
Goodbye, au revoir,
farewell,
farewell!

Papa loves to call me Punch,
his favorite crunch,
the toughest kid of all the bunch.

He'll grab my wrist and make a fist
and then insist I punch his head
and then pretend that he is dead.

But then he'll say,
"You win, okay,
'cause you're my Punch,
my favorite crunch,
the toughest kid of
all the bunch!"

The room was filled with smoke and sweat.
The fight was still not over yet.
And there stood Punch, that favorite crunch,
the toughest kid of all the bunch.

But then—oh, wow!
Oh, holy cow!
The next contender took a bow.
Her biceps looked as strong as steel.
Her triceps looked so huge! Unreal!

And as for Punch,
she had a hunch—
she was the competition's lunch!

Dear Dad
is fond of Eleanora.
He says, "It's grand
with so much mora.

But then—oh, wow!
Oh, holy cow!
The next contender took a bow.
Her biceps looked as strong as steel.
Her triceps looked so huge! Unreal!

And as for Punch,
she had a hunch—
she was the competition's lunch!

Dear Dad
is fond of Eleanora.
He says, "It's grand
with so much mora.

My Eleanora will go far,
a singer and a movie star."

The fans adora
Ms. Eleanora,
the movie star
with so much mora.
And when she sings
her voice can soara,

and when she acts
her fans just roara.
They clap and cheer
and stamp the floora.

And when she bows the fans implora,
"Encora! Encora!" for Eleanora!

Then when she's tired she cries, "No mora!
I need a break from Eleanora!"

Now Mom is going through a phase,
a kind of NAME INVENTION CRAZE.
She's come up with a hundred ways
that folks can say my name.

It's somewhat
of a mystery
what drives
this creativity.
With all these names
it might just be
Mom hasn't found
the name that's me.

The gourmet critic Don Rissoni
will dine tonight at Ellatony.
The chef?
Miss Elbow Macaroni.

He sniffed her
Pasta Rigatoni.
He whiffed her
light Zabaglione.

And then the
famous
Don Rissoni

I often call up Great Aunt Bertie,
who changed her name when she was thirty.
She says she's glad because she had
the longest name she's ever seen:
Begonia Eucalyptus Rose Tulip Iris Evergreen!

Aunt Bertie seems to understand
how things can get way out of hand
when grown-ups take a name too far
and leave you wondering who you are.

Aunt Bertie says,
"These little nicknames come and go.
Folks give them 'cause they love you so.
The day will come when you will know
the name that's right for you!"

That day did come.

It was a bright Thanksgiving Day.
At least it started out that way.
But in between the fun and games
the grown-ups started with *my* names.

First Papa's calling for his Punch.
He needs to hug his favorite crunch.
While *Nana's* calling for her Elle,
her pretty, poised mademoiselle,
Dad sings a song called
"Eleanora, Movie Star with
           so Much Mora."

And as Mom makes the pumpkin pie,
she's shouting names.
We hear her cry.
"Oh, Ellenshake!
Oh, Ellenbake!
Oh, how I love my Ellencake!"

Then . . .

Mom goes quiet for a while
and suddenly begins to smile.
A light goes on inside her head.
She looks at me. Here's what she said:

"E!
We'll call you E.
It's just so wee," says Mom to Dad.
"The cutest name she's ever had!"
And gee–they seemed to be so glad,
that I just had one thing to add.

My family's gone completely mad!
E's not a name.
E's not a word.
It's just a letter.
It's absurd!
The dumbest thing I've ever heard!

Enough, enough
with all this stuff!
These games with names—
I've had enough!
Who's Elbow Mac?
Please take it back!
Miss Eleanora, Ellencake—
Don't use those names.
They just sound fake!
Along with Elle and Punch and E,
they are NOT the girl you see.
There is a girl I want to be,
and there's a name
that's right for me.

So that is how I overcame
the many problems with my name.
And on that day my name became:

ELLIE!

Each member of my family
thinks Ellie suits me perfectly
and absolutely all agree . . .

Ellie is the girl they see.
Ellie is the girl I'll be.
Ellie is the name for me!